Meet The Super Six . . .

Hi! I'm Gus.
I'm the oldest and biggest,
so I'm the ... Duh! ...
Whatchacallit? ... the Fiver!

You're the Sixer, Gus!
Hello, everyone! I'm Jane.
I like everything stylish and cute!

Yo, dudes!
My name's Martin,
but everyone calls me Ice
'cos I'm So Cool!

Hello, you guys!
I'm Joe Kerr by name
and joker by nature!

Greetings! I'm Brenda.
I'm often called 'Little Miss Perfect'
because I always get everything right!

Hi, everybody! I'm Sammy!
I've just joined this Six from the Beaver Scouts
and they're all really nice to me - except they
call me 'Titch'!

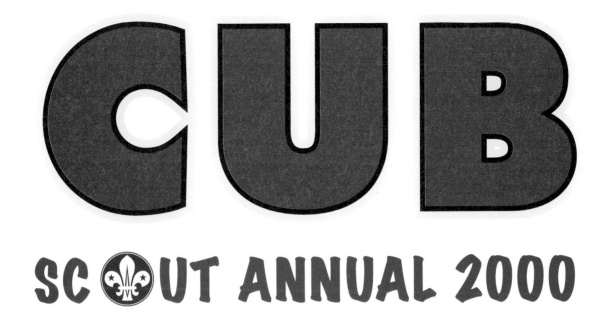

CUB

SCOUT ANNUAL 2000

Pedigree

BOOKS

The Old Rectory, Matford Lane, Exeter, Devon EX2 4PS
Printed in Germany. ISBN 1-902836-10-3

£6.99

CS.1

CUB

SCOUTS CONTENTS

The Beast of Bodkin Moor - Strip story 7

Super Six Puzzle Parade - Ice's Cool and Not Cool Conundrums 12

The Old Jokes Home 14

Photo Feature 15

Exotic Pets - We Do Like Spiders 18

Feature - Over the Hills and Far Away 21

Butlins - A Great Day Out 26

Competition 26

Super Six Puzzle Parade - Brenda's Wordsearch Challenge 32

The Old Jokes Home 34

Mr Kipling Makes..."Exceedingly Good Books" 35

Writers Badge - No Arithmetic! 38

Story - "I'm the Leader of the Gang, I am" 41

Come and Join Us! 44

Super Six Puzzle Parade - Gus's Horrible Homework Howlers 46

The Old Jokes Home 48

The World's Best Paper Plane 49

Strip Story - A Week in the Life of The Super Six 52

Photo Feature 56

Scoutmaster Snoopy 61

How to Gain Your Artist Badge 65

Super Six Puzzle Parade - Sammy's Giant Wordsnake 68

The Old Jokes Home 70

Exotic Pets - We Do Like Snakes 71

Superstar Recipes 74

The Adventure Crest Award 77

The Old Jokes Home 81

Super Six Puzzle Parade - Jane's Generation Gap Triple Puzzle 82

Story - Sammy's Good Turn 84

Photo Feature 87

Give Me the Monet 90

Monet's Colouring Picture 93

How to Gain Your Gardening Badge 95

Super Six Puzzle Parade - Joe's Riddle of the Sands 98

The Old Jokes Home 100

Strip Story - All Manor of Surprises 101

National Competition Report 106

The Lowdown on Becoming a Scout 108

Super Six Puzzle Parade

Ice's Cool And Not-Cool Conundrums

Stand by for some advice from Ice!

Listed below are some of the things which Ice considers cool.
Fit them into the grid, using the letters already in place to help you.
Then the middle section, reading downwards, will spell out what Ice considers
Coolest of all!

Trainers	**Scouting**	**Boxing**
Rapping	**Sweatshirts**	**Rock 'N Roll**
Go Karts	**Skateboards**	**Swimming**
Jeans	**Shades**	**Boomboxes**

TO BE COOL OR UNCOOL - THAT IS THE QUESTION!

Now solve this Coded Message to find what Ice thinks is Not cool. The numbers refer to the letters in the grid opposite.

"In my opinion, it is totally uncool to be …

1	2	3	4

,

5	6	7	4

,

8	9	5	10	11	12

,

12	5	2	8	8	10	11	12

,

6	11	13	10	11	7

AND

14	4	2	11

!

All Good Clean Fun

ULP! Think I just trod on a hippo!

Photograph: Tim Burgess

Found It!

Photograph: Scott Hamilton

This couldn't be better – unless it was chocolate!

Photograph: Tim Burgess

Watch The Birdie

Did you just try to bite my ear? *

So you don't like my face paint? Well we don't give two hoots!*

Who are you calling a twit – twoo?

*Photographs: Chris Boardman

Why do I always get the small one?*

Climb Every Mountain

OOO-ER! This bit's coming loose!

Photograph: Paul Dudley

If I'd known what this would do to my finger nails I would never have volunteered!

Photograph: Kevin Cook

Hey! It's easier coming down than going up!

Photograph: M. Le Riche

We Do Like

How To Keep Tarantulas

Scientists have suggested that human beings may be born with a built-in fear of spiders and snakes. Certainly, very many people run a mile at the sight of a big spider and shudder with revulsion at the thought of handling a snake. This is a great pity because most members of both species are quite harmless and are creatures of great delicacy and beauty.

Years ago, people believed that if you were bitten by a tarantula, you would do a crazy dance and then die. This is just not true. Though there are some very poisonous tarantulas, they tend to live far away in the Amazon Rain Forest and are quite different from the non-poisonous varieties sold in pet shops. Even these can give you a nasty bite, but that is if they are not treated properly. Handled well, a tame tarantula will make a super pet - easy to keep, amazingly cheap to buy and feed, and really cool to look at!

BUYING

Like everything else, the price of a tarantula varies enormously, but you should be able to find one that costs in the region of £20. This is not a lot of money, given that your new pet is likely to live for a good 10 years. In fact, you'll probably find that the cost of setting up your vivarium (the place where your spider lives) will cost considerably more than the animal itself!

The most popular types of tarantula to choose from are:

The Mexican Red-Knee (*Euathlus Smithi*)
Often called *'The Mexican Red-leg'*

- large
- black and orange
- hairy
- normally placid and good-natured.

SPIDERS!

The Chilean Rose (*Grammostola Cala*)
Also known as *'The Chilean Beautiful'*

- chocolate brown with cream-coloured hairs and a pink tummy
  - more nervous and aggressive.

HOUSING

Tarantulas do not need a great deal of space in which to live, so a medium-sized fish tank is ideal for them. Glass sides are better than plastic because they are easier to clean and do not discolour. Because they are not filled with water, your aquarium does not need to be leak proof - but it must be escape proof! (You don't want to find your pet beside you on the pillow!) So make sure your tank has a lid that fits properly. Fill your tank with gravel or potting compost, but not soil from the garden as this could contain parasites. Spiders like a piece of log to hide under and attach their webs to. And a backdrop picture, attached to the rear wall of your tank, can make a realistic-looking desert or mountain scene.

LIGHTING AND HEATING

Your spider is from a tropical region and has no bodily mechanism to regulate heat - so it must be kept really warm at all times. Have a light on during the day and a heat-pad on at night. Find out the temperature that your particular species likes best and keep to it, using a thermometer on the outside of the tank to guide you.

19

The Tarantula

- Tarantulas are named after the town of Taranto in Italy, home of the European tarantula known as 'Wolf Spider'.
- The largest tarantulas of all are the "bird-eating" spiders of South America - so called because they actually eat small birds! Their leg span is in the region of 28 cm!
- Despite having 8 eyes, tarantulas have quite poor eyesight. They rely mainly on touch to sense what is around them.
- As well as poison and sharp fangs, many tarantulas defend themselves by shooting their hairs at an attacker which can prove very painful and irritating.
- Tarantulas are solitary creatures. You cannot keep two together in a tank because they will fight. Also, when mating, the female will often attack the male.
- Female tarantulas live considerably longer than males. Even those bred in captivity, the female lives for about 12 years whereas the male only lasts about 6. In the wild, a female can live up to 30 years whereas a male is lucky to live past 5!

FEEDING

This is the bit that might put you off owning a tarantula. They have to be fed live prey! But this is not as bad as it seems. The most common food is crickets which are bred specially for the purpose and can be bought at pet shops for about 5 pence each. You just bring them home in a plastic bag, shake them into the tank and leave them for your spider to find and pounce on when hungry. And don't forget a water bowl. Keep it small and maybe put a piece of sponge in it to prevent your tarantula from drowning.

MOULTING

Unlike a snake, which just sheds its skin, tarantulas shed their whole outer shells (called the 'exoskeleton'). This is obviously a very difficult time for your spider and it is important to avoid handling or disturbance when this is happening. A successful moult leaves you with a complete skin which looks just like another spider - so don't fall into the trap of mistaking it for your pet and thinking he is dead!

Over The Hills And Far Away!

MOUNTAIN BIKES RULE!

Want to be trendier than Jane or cooler than Ice?
All you need to do is get a mountain bike, a good helmet and set off into the wild, blue yonder!

Not long ago, mountain bikes did not exist. If you wanted to do some serious cycling, you had to buy a racing bike which was only suitable for riding on the roads. Now with all the new designs and technology, you have the freedom to go anywhere - on road or across country. It's a whole new world ... and it's waiting for you to explore it!

Of course, like everything else that is exciting and fun, mountain biking is potentially dangerous. So here are a few handy hints on how to do it properly ...

DO

USE YOUR HEAD - WEAR A HELMET!

Believe it or not, it could happen to you! However confident you are, or however careful you are, you will probably at some time fall off your bike. And when you do, you need to be wearing something to protect your most precious asset - your head!

Cycle helmets really can lessen the pain and damage caused by a bang on the head - you only have to ask those wearing them when they fell off (and those that were not!)

Always make sure your helmet is the right size for you and fits properly. And buy a good one. They are recognised as conforming to British Standards and they carry these marks:
BS6863, AS2063, ANSIZ 90.4 or SNELL.

KEEP 'EM CLEAN AND BE SEEN

The law says that your bicycle must have a white light at the front and a red light and red reflector at the back. And it's not only illegal to ignore this requirement - it's also downright silly! Motorists can't see you properly if you don't have lights and you're in great danger of being knocked over.

If you go splashing through puddles and skidding through mud, remember to clean your lights before you go out at night. And do make sure to change your batteries regularly. A front light that looks like a candle on the horizon is no use to anybody!

Don't

ROUTE OF THE PROBLEM

Like having no lights, it is illegal to cycle on the pavement, go through red lights or down a one-way street the wrong way. So don't do it! Not only is it dangerous for you, it puts other people at risk, too.

Similarly, if you are cycling off-road in the park or elsewhere, where you share the track with pedestrians, make sure you don't go by too fast and scare people or - worse still - collide with younger children. You can go extremely fast on a mountain bike and do a lot of damage if you hit somebody.

For your own safety, it's always best to avoid main roads if you can. Use the side streets or cycle lanes where they exist.

DON'T BE MEAN WITH YOUR MEAN MACHINE

Do make sure you look after your bike. Brakes and tyres are the parts which wear out the quickest, so check them regularly and 'replace your rubber' sooner rather than later.

It's amazing what a difference a few squirts of oil can make to the performance of your bike! Oil the chain, wheels and other moving parts regularly and you'll speed along like a silent bird! If a major fault develops, get it fixed properly by a grown-up or your local bike shop. It's worth maintaining your mountain bike properly. Chances are, it cost quite a bit in the first place and it will last much longer (and be more resalable) if you look after it.

Finally, never overload your bike or try to carry heavy loads on it (especially with something dangling that could catch in the wheels). Use a saddlebag, panniers or a backpack.

The Raleigh DHO

And now, prepare to have your breath taken away! Your dad may drool over a Ferrari, your older brother may give his eye-teeth for a Yamaha motorbike, but here's the mountain bike you'd die for ...

SPECIFICATION

Rockshox Boxxer PRO - 151mm of progressive travel gives shattering all-round performance on any kind of hits. Coil-springs and tunable HydraCoil technology damping.

Rockshox Super Delux - Big Daddy of shockers. Smooth and super-charged. Comes with separate external compression and rebound damping. Enjoy your flight.

PRODUCT TYPE	Downhill
FRAME	Reynolds 853
GEARS	9
FORK	Rockshox Boxxer Pro
SHOCK	RS Super Deluxe

The Ultimate

CONT...

HEADSET	Chris King
CHAINSET	XTR
RR MECH	ESP 9.0SL
SHIFTERS	ESP 9.0SL
BRAKES	Hope disc
LEVERS	Hope disc
CASSETTE	Deore XT 9 speed
HUB	Deemax
TYRES	Continental Vertical Pro
STEM	Azonic shorty
BARS	Azonic double wall
GRIPS	WTB dual compound
SADDLE	X-Lite kevlar
SEAT POST	X-Lite Clikon
PEDALS	Wellgo WAM 1DH
COLOUR	Boxxer red/black
SIZES	Small and Medium
PRICE GUIDE	£3,999.99

Dream Machine!

We would like to thank Ben Bread and James Dewdeswell of the Raleigh Cycle Centre, Worthing, for their help in preparing this feature. Photographs and information kindly supplied by Raleigh Industries Ltd, Nottingham. For further details, telephone 0115 942 0202.

A Great

If you're looking for somewhere exciting to go next summer, you couldn't do better than the new Butlins Family Entertainment Resorts. They're at Skegness in Lincolnshire, Minehead in Somerset and Bognor Regis in West Sussex - so there's one within reasonable travelling distance for a large part of the country. Each resort is packed with wonderful things to do, so you won't know where to start first!

COMPETITION TIME

Even more exciting, though, is the news that Butlins have very kindly offered some fantastic prizes for Beaver Scouts and Cub Scouts. If you're the lucky winner of the competition in the Cub Scout Annual , you'll win a day's free entry for your Beaver Scout Colony - that's 36 children and 7 adults! Not only that, if you visit Butlins with your family and you produce the badge printed at the end of this feature, you will also get in Free provided you are accompanied by one paying grown-up!

Is that cool, or what?!

Full details of the competition and token can be found later on. First, let's look at some (and only some) of the fantastic attractions awaiting you at Butlins ...

The centrepiece of each Butlins resort is the brand new weatherproof Skyline Pavilion. This huge structure (it's as big as the football pitch at Wembley Stadium!) has a see-through roof like a Circus Big Top and see-through walls, some 40 feet high!, so it feels like you're outdoors when you're indoors. And, of course, it doesn't matter if it's pouring with rain because you won't get wet! Beneath the Skyline's vast canopy, there's a whole world of entertainment for visitors to enjoy. The indoor streets are packed with cafes, restaurants and take-away snack bars - complete with amazing Live Entertainment. The acts form a magical mixture of fantasy, illusion and circus skills. The Circus Parade is led by the Conjurer, a master of baffling magic tricks. You'll meet The Storyteller who loves nothing better than telling stories to children, except when he's being annoyed by playful Word the Worm! Then there's the Puppet Master, calling children to his amazing Magic Toy Shop and to see his full-sized puppets appearing on stage. High above, you'll see the death-defying stunts of trapeze artists from a proper circus. And finally there are midweek live appearances by your favourite Fox Kids TV characters including the X-men, Casper and the awesome Power Rangers Turbo!

Welcome to The Pleasure Dome

Day Out!

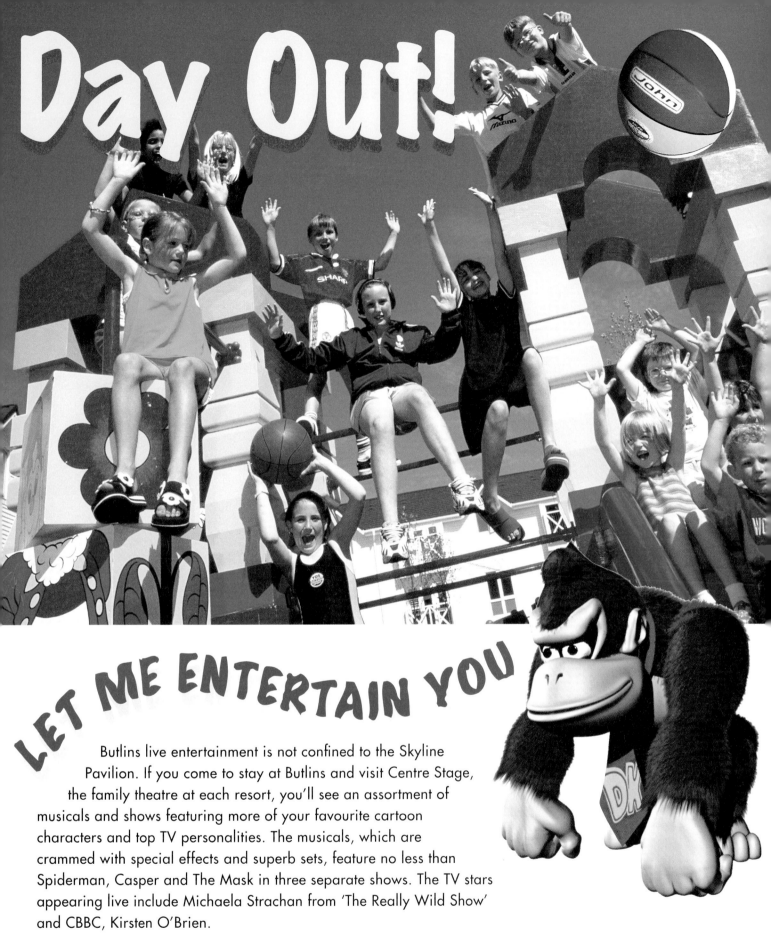

LET ME ENTERTAIN YOU

Butlins live entertainment is not confined to the Skyline Pavilion. If you come to stay at Butlins and visit Centre Stage, the family theatre at each resort, you'll see an assortment of musicals and shows featuring more of your favourite cartoon characters and top TV personalities. The musicals, which are crammed with special effects and superb sets, feature no less than Spiderman, Casper and The Mask in three separate shows. The TV stars appearing live include Michaela Strachan from 'The Really Wild Show' and CBBC, Kirsten O'Brien.

Okay, so you've sat on the coach to get there; you've sat in the Pavilion to eat and drink, now its time to get active! Nobody knows better than Butlins how much children enjoy doing things!

At all three resorts, there's a mouth watering array of activities on offer for energetic youngsters aged 5 and upwards (and that includes Beaver Scouts and Cub Scouts). And remember, once you're inside, the majority are absolutely free.

So Much To Do ... And So Little TIME!

Sports fanatics can play all day on the superb, all-weather multi-sports courts. You can choose to play soccer, netball, basketball, volleyball or tennis.

If you prefer a slightly gentler game, there's a championship length bowling green so you can show Grandad what he's been doing wrong for all these years. And if golf is your game, why not test your skills on the colourful crazy golf course?

Everyone loves the Funfair and it's a tradition that Butlins are proud to continue. The fair at each resort has all your favourite rides including dodgems, waltzers and the carousel, as well as a host of other exciting attractions.

Finally, new of 1999, are the Fox Kids 'Rumble In the Jungle' adventure play areas.

Featuring three fantastic themes - Donkey Kong Country, Ninja Turtles and the Adventures of Mowgli - these state-of-the-art outdoor playgrounds will give you the climbs, slides and swings of a lifetime!

WATER Wonderful World

No day-trip to Butlins would be complete without a visit to the swimming pool. Butlins have always been at the forefront of water-based fun and the latest water rides, and their new sub-tropical Splash Waterworld is no exception. This fantastic swimming complex boasts a wavepool, wonderful waterfalls and the very latest water rides from America. Try the Space Bowl, an incredible 40 mph spin around a giant bowl, ending with a dramatic splashdown in view of your family or Leaders. Or how about the Master Blaster? This gravity-defying water experience for two people takes your double-raft on a 10 metre drop from the launch tower, then blasts you right back to the top again for a breathtaking 200 metre roller-coaster ride to the finish!

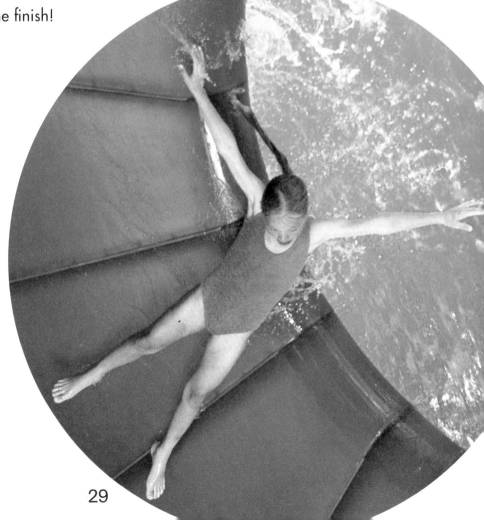

If you don't like this rough-stuff, or are too small for it, remember there are always the shallow-play areas where you can swim or splash about in the lovely clear, blue water.

So, having whetted your appetite for a day out at Butlins, now's your chance to win one in the Summer of the year 2000 for yourself and your Cub Scout Colony.

Cub Scout Annual 2000

Competition Question

1. What was the name of the island, in Poole Harbour in Dorset, where Lord Baden-Powell ran his first Scout Camp in 1907?

2. In what year were the Wolf Cubs started as a separate Section for younger boys?

3. What is the day, month and year of Lord Baden-Powell's birthday?

If you think you know the answers to these three questions, write them down on the entry form opposite. Then fill in the tie-breaker section, saying why you love being a Cub Scout. Finally, fill in the details about yourself and cut out the entry form.
(You can photocopy it if you don't want to spoil your annual).
Send it to this address:

> **Cub Scout Annual 2000 Competition**
> **The Scout Association**
> **Baden-Powell House**
> **Queen's Gate**
> **London SW7 5JS**

And please don't forget to put a stamp on your envelope.
The Post Office won't deliver any unstamped mail.

Closing date for entries: Tuesday February 29th, 2000
(That's an easy one to remember - it's Leap Year day!)

After the closing date, all the correct entries will be put into a big box and thoroughly shaken about.
Then one form will be picked out completely at random.
The lucky winner will be informed by post sometime in the Spring. Free tickets for his or her Cub Scout Pack (36 chidren and 7 accompanying adults) will then be sent in time for a great day out in the Summer.

Details of the winner and possibly of the day out itself will be published in next year's Cub Scout Annual.

Cub Scout Annual 2000 Competition

1. Lord Baden-Powell held his first Scout Camp on _____ Island.

2. The Wolf Cubs were started in _____

3. Lord Baden-Powell's birthday is _____

I like being a Cub Scout because _____
(No more than 20 words)

_____

_____

_____

My name is: _____

My age is: _____

My home address is: _____

_____

My Cub Scout Pack is: _____

Rules of Entry You do not need to have bought the Cub Scout Annual 2000 to enter.
Entries limited to one per person. The decision of the Selection Panel is final.
No person connected with the production of the Cub Scout Annual 2000 is allowed to enter.

Cub Scout Annual 2000 Badge
FREE INDIVIDUAL ENTRY BADGE

If you don't win the competition, don't despair! You can still enjoy a day-trip to Butlins absolutely free if you are accompanied by one paying grown-up and you produce this badge. This time, of course, a photocopy won't be acceptable. So you can either cut the coupon out or take the whole annual with you to show at the gate.

Which ever way you go, you're bound to have fun. Butlins is an ideal place for families!

This badge entitles you to free entry to Butlins for one day when accompanied by a paying adult.

Super Six Puzzle Parade

Brenda's Wordsearch Challenge

Being a bit of a boffin, it only took Brenda 10 minutes to complete this wordsearch and work out the follow-on section below. Can you do better than that?

Here are 21 words which are all to do with the Cub Scouts. They are hidden in the grid opposite, spelt in all directions including backwards. When you have found and marked off all the words, transfer the remaining letters in order into the boxes below. They will spell a very special name.

What is it?

Pack	Handshake	Investiture	Grand Howl
Badges	Prize	Promise	Adventures
Camping	Woggle	Church	Uniform
		Challenge	Flag
		Akela	Scarf
		Sports	First Aid
		Fun	Six
			Salute

Bet you can't beat me!

32

C	H	A	L	L	E	N	G	E	L	O	S
A	I	U	R	D	B	E	K	A	D	T	D
M	E	N	W	A	L	N	C	I	R	S	P
P	O	I	V	G	W	E	A	O	E	L	H
I	R	F	G	E	L	T	P	R	F	W	A
N	L	O	O	F	S	S	U	R	E	O	N
G	W	R	M	R	X	T	A	Z	H	H	D
A	A	M	I	I	N	C	I	G	C	D	S
L	L	F	S	E	S	R	I	T	R	N	H
F	E	L	V	W	P	E	E	L	U	A	A
L	K	D	S	A	L	U	T	E	H	R	K
B	A	D	G	E	S	N	U	F	C	G	E

| | | | | | | | | | | - | | | | | | | | |

| | | | | | | | | |

Special Activity Feature

Learn about the man who created the names used by Cub Scout Leaders and gain your Book Reader or Writer Badge ...

Mr Kipling Makes ...
Exceedingly Good Books

Rudyard Kipling has a special place in the hearts of Cub Scouts everywhere. It was he who wrote the famous children's story, 'The Jungle Book', from which Lord Baden-Powell took names like 'Akela' to give to Leaders of his newly-formed Wolf Cub packs.

Here's a short introduction to this well-known novelist, short story writer and poet ...

35

UNHAPPY CHILDHOOD

Joseph Rudyard Kipling was born on December 30th, 1865, in Bombay, India. His mother and father were upper-class English officials with connections to the British government.

At the age of six, Kipling was taken to England and left with foster parents in Southsea near Portsmouth. He was very unhappy there. Later, he was moved to a second-rate boarding school in north Devon. The bullying of his fellow pupils and the beatings from the teachers meant he was even unhappier there.

COLOURFUL INDIA

In 1882, at the age of 17, Kipling returned to India where he worked as a journalist. He was fascinated by the colour and bustle of India and, in his spare time, began writing poems and short stories about what he saw around him. Eventually, they were published and proved to be extremely popular with readers in England. Back home, in 1890, he suddenly found himself acclaimed as the best writer of his age!

Akela
the leader of the wolf pack

Chil
the bird of prey

Hathi
the elephant

AMERICA AND 'THE JUNGLE BOOK'

In 1892, Kipling married a young American girl called Caroline Balestier and the couple moved to house in Vermont, USA. They did not settle there. The neighbours did not like them - and Kipling di not like the neighbours! (He was always very pro-British and tended to look down upon other people!) Even so, during this unsettled time America, Kipling wrote some of his best works including 'The Jungle Books' in 1894 and 1895. The stories of Mowgli, the "wolf-boy"; Baloo, the friendly bear; Bagheera, the sinister black par the leader of the pack have become classics, inspiring not only Baden-Powell, but also countless generations of children - including Walt Disney who turned the stories into a colourful musical cartoon film in the 1960's.

Baloo
the friendly bear

In 1902, Rudyard Kipling returned to England once more. This time, he was to stay, buying a house in Sussex where he lived until his death on January 18th, 1936.

Kipling reached the height of his fame during these later years of his life. In 1907 he was awarded The Nobel Prize for Literature, one of the highest honours a writer can achieve. He accepted this award, but for some reason, twice turned down a medal called The Order Of Merit which is generally regarded as one of the top awards which can be given to a British citizen.

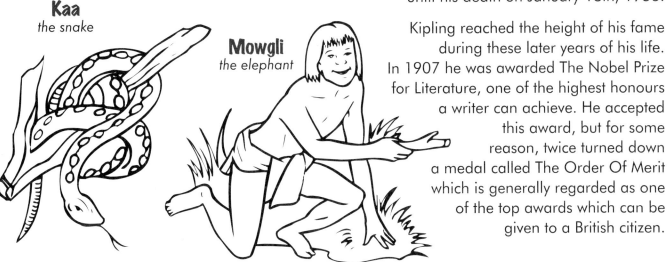

Kaa
the snake

Mowgli
the elephant

Raksa
the mother wolf

Rama
the leader of buffaloes

Finally, mention must be made of one of Kipling's poems which has also become as famous as be is. It is called "IF" and begins:

'If you can keep your head
when all about you
are losing theirs and
blaming it on you ...'

and finishes:

...'You'll be a man, my son!'

Bagheera
the black panther

This much-quoted poem (most people only know the above lines, not the middle!) sums up Kipling's attitude to life very well. He believed in hard work, discipline, helping others - very much the Cubs' philosophy. No wonder Lord Baden-Powell chose him to be part of his great Scouting venture!

NO ARITHMETIC!

How To Gain Your Book Reader Badge and Writer Badge

Now here are some suggestions about how to choose the books you read and go about presenting your findings to the examiner …

Here's the official list of requirements for gaining the Book Reader Badge…

1. Produce a list of at least 6 books you have read or used recently, name their authors and be able to tell the examiner something about three of the books. The three books to be chosen by you are to include at least one story and at least one factual book.
(Note: The three books must be of a reasonable standard, taking the Cub Scout's age and development into account.)
2. Show that you understand how to care for books.
3. Show that you can use a dictionary, encyclopedia and an atlas.
4. Explain to the examiner how the books in a library are set out and how to find fiction and non-fiction books.

■ When you're in the library or bookshop, look at the front cover of a book first. You may well have heard of the title or the author. Don't always be swayed by appearances - a book with an exciting cover picture may be boring or difficult to read, and a dull one may be very exciting!

■ Look at the back cover of the book you are choosing. This often gives you a brief summary of the storyline and tells you what the book is about. This can be a very useful guide for deciding if it's for you.

■ Finally, look inside the book. It may have a contents page or list of chapter headings. These are further guides. And look at the size of the print and the language used - is it too baby or too grown-up for you?

Some Cubs inspired by reading the stories of King Arthur and his Knights Of The Round Table …

When you face the examiner for your Book Reader Badge, he or she is likely to ask you the following questions to find out if you have read the books properly. So why not be a true Cub Scout and Be Prepared!

FOR STORY BOOKS

- What is the title and who is the author?
- What type of story is it - adventure, comedy, mystery and so on?
- Who are the main characters?
- Where and when does the story take place?
- What were the best parts of the story?

FOR FACTUAL BOOKS

- What is the title?
- What is the subject of the book?
- Which parts are the most interesting or useful?

Now let's move on to the Writer Badge.

Here's the official list of requirements for gaining the Writer Badge...

1. Make and present a collection of stories and/or poems you have written on a variety of themes.
2. Write a report on a recent Cub Scout event for use in a newsletter or magazine and read it to others.
3. Write a letter and address an envelope neatly, and show a knowledge of postcodes and letter postal rates: e.g. a thank you letter, an invitation, a request for help, a letter to a friend, or any other suitable subject.

"I'm certainly going to write about this in my report of our Pack visit to London".

Finally, here are some suggestions about how you can go about tackling your Writer Badge...

- You could write a straightforward story about one group of characters that you have made up. (It would need to be several pages long.)

- You could write a collection of stories about different characters each time.

- You could write a story for younger children and illustrate it. This could look exciting if you mount it on a long, zig-zag shaped piece of cardboard which unfolds and stands up.

- You could write a factual report of something you did with the Cubs (such as a Fun Day or Scout Camp) or with your family (such as a holiday or special outing.)

- You could report on an item of local news or interest. Go and interview people and quote what they say. If you want to feel really professional, you could record your interviews on a tape recorder and type up your report on a proper typewriter or computer.

- You could become official "letter writer" for your Six, sending thank you letters to places you have visited with your Pack or people who helped out at Camp. This will teach you the right way to set out a letter and how to use post codes correctly.

- You could find yourself a pen pal and write lots of letters to him or her. If you manage to locate another Cub Scout about your age in another part of the country, not only will you have a friend who shares your interests, but also both of you can work for your Writer Badge at the same time!

"We visited "Mexico", these fantastic gardens in Jersey in the Channel Islands ..."

The Super Six in
"I'm The Leader Of The Gang, I Am!"

"There's no way", said Jane, "that we can let Gus lead us on this Orienteering Challenge this afternoon."

"I agree," added Joe. "Gus gets lost coming out of his house and going down the path to the front gate!"

"He's going to be mighty upset when we tell him we don't want him as leader," commented Ice. "And there's also the problem of who's going to take his place."

"The letter is not a problem!" exclaimed Brenda. "The obvious person to lead this Six is Me!"

The Super Six were at Summer Camp, miles from civilisation. The Orienteering afternoon looked a bit daunting, involving a long trek over the open moors with only a map and a compass for guidance. Jane and the others were still debating what to do about Gus when he arrived with Sammy.

"Look what I've made this morning," cried Sammy, holding up a model boat made with matchsticks. Gus's eyes filed up and everyone thought he was going to cry like a big softie! But Gus was going to sneeze!

"Atishoo!" he bellowed, blowing Sammy's boat to smithereens.

"Have you caught a cold, Gus?" asked Jane.

"Yeb," said Gus. "By dose is all blocked up. Gotta go to bed ... Atishoooo!"

"Problem solved!" said Ice.

There was no arguing with Brenda, and so the five Cub Scouts set off on their Challenge with her in the lead.

"I hope Little Miss Perfect know what she's doing," murmured Joe from the back of the line.

"I heard that!" called Brenda. "Of course I know what I'm doing! Have you ever known me to do anything wrong?"

"My legs are starting to ache," said Sammy.

"Don't start that again, Titch!" cried Ice.

The group walked for a long time in silence. The only person who spoke was Brenda, pointing and saying "This way!" at regular intervals. After a while, Joe began to suspect something had gone wrong.

"I reckon we're walking round in circles!" he cried.

"Nonsense!" snapped Brenda.

"Yes, we are!" agreed Jane. "This is the third time we've walked past that tree with the broken branch."

Then Ice noticed the map Brenda was holding. He snatched it out of her hand.

"You've brought the wrong one!" he exclaimed. "This is a map of Scotland!"

"Everyone makes mistakes," said Brenda, meekly.

Ice and Joe took over the leadership of the Six.

"Follow us, guys," called Joe, looking t his compass. "If we walk due East for the next half an hour, we should arrive at the next Rendezvous Point."

So everyone tramped over the springy moorland grass for half an hour … and another half an hour … and another!"

"My legs really ache!" wailed Sammy.

"So do mine now," agreed Ice. "Where are we?"

"We're lost, that's where we are!" cried Jane, pointing to the compass in Joe's hand.

"That thing's busted! Look at the needle - it's going round and round in circles!"

"Oh, great!" said Brenda. "So we're stuck in the middle of the wilderness with no map and no compass!"

Suddenly, Jane remembered that she had put some binoculars in her backpack.

"I can use these to spot the other Sixes doing the Challenge!" she cried. "If we follow them, they'll lead us home."

The idea worked well. Jane caught a glimpse of some fellow Cub Scouts in the distance and everyone set off in pursuit. With Jane leading them, our friends almost completed the course … but then they ran into a problem.

"It's getting dark!" cried Jane. "I can't see anything any more!"

Darkness closed in very quickly on the moors. Everyone had torches, of course, but they were like little pinpricks of light against the huge, inky blackness of the sky.

"I wish I was tucked up in my tent with Akela saying goodnight to me!" wailed Sammy.

"Don't be such a baby …" began Brenda.

"I wish it, too!" yelled Joe.

"Shhh!" hissed Ice, urgently.

"W-w-what is it?" gulped Jane. "An owl? A bat? A horrible creepy T-t-thing!"

"No," replied Ice, coolly. "It's a sneeze!"

Everyone fell silent and listened intently. Sure enough, moments later, a feint "Atishoo!" could be heard in the far distance.

"Gus!" cried everyone, together.

By following the sound of the sneezes, which occurred in great frequency and increasing volume, the group found their way back to camp!

The following morning, Brenda led the others round to the medical tent to thank Gus.

"Don't know what we would have done without you last night," said Brenda, shaking Gus's hand warmly. "You got us home safely, like a true Sixer, and we always want you to lead us!"

"Eh?" said Gus. "Ahh … Ahhh … Ahhhhtishooo!"

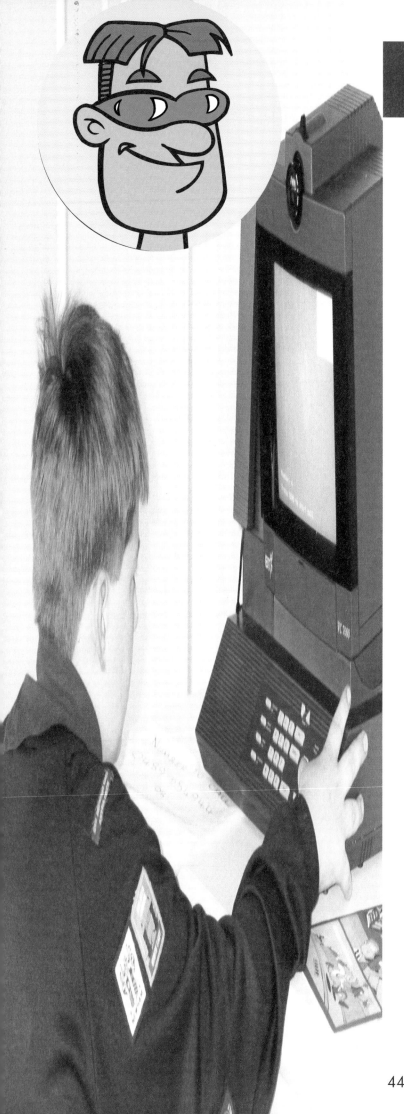

An introduction to Scoutbase UK - The Scouts' own website on the Internet!

Calling all computer buffs (and anyone else interested in the way we'll all be getting in touch with each other in the 21st Century!). Here's a very brief history of how The Scout Association's official website came about and what you can get from it if you use it.

COMMUNICATIONS 'R' US!

Scouts have always been keen on communication. In the early days, you learned how to send messages using flags (semaphore) or with the dots and dashes of Morse Code. So it is no wonder that the Scout Movement is at the forefront of the new technology which offers quicker and easier communication than ever before.

SCOUTBASE UK RULES

In the early 1990s, a small group of Scout Leaders began using their computers to exchange ideas and information with other Scouts around the world. At first, they worked separately; then, they pooled their ideas, calling their newly-formed group 'Scoutbase UK'. They showed the Scout Association the range of services that could be offered to Scouts via the Internet and, before long, Scoutbase UK became the official Scouting website.

All this was way ahead of its time. Scoutbase was one of the first computer organisations in the UK, if not the world!

FULFILLING THE DREAM

In the first couple of years, an average of 3,000 people a day visited the Scoutbase UK website. Since then, the figure has risen to 5,000 a day - and will doubtless continue to rise as more Scouts link up with the Net.

The statistics also show that about half of the visitors are UK Scouts - the other half come from abroad (from approx. 100 different countries, in fact). So this modern technology is going a long way towards fulfilling Lord Baden-Powell's dream of a truly international Movement in which Scouts can make friends with each other from all around the world!

WHAT'S ON OFFER?

Well, there's almost anything you can think of - the latest Newsletter from Scout HQ, information about Scouts in other countries, programme ideas, information about the different sections of the Scout Movement etc. And other related websites can give you access to a Scout bookshop, camp site reviews, fact sheets and a calendar of forthcoming events. In fact, there is an ever-growing list of information, goods and services that you can obtain through your computer!

SITES TO ACCESS

Finally, here are the names and e-mail addresses of some of the main Internet websites you can access:

ScoutBase UK	http://www.scoutbase.org.uk
ScoutNet UK	http:///www.scoutnet.org.uk
The Spider's Web	http://www.spider.scout.net
Scouting Magazine	http://www.enterprise.net/scouting magazine

With special thanks to Chris Atkinson for the information in this feature.

GUS'S HORRIBLE HOMEWORK HOWLERS

Oh, dear! In order to get to his Pack Meeting on time, Gus has rushed his homework! Instead of looking up the correct answers, he has taken wild guesses - and got it all wrong!

Can you help? Here are 15 well-known proverbs.
When you've had a good giggle at Gus's daft ideas, write the correct endings in the spaces underneath.

1. **The early bird catches the flu.**

2. **Don't put all your eggs in one omelette.**

3. **All's fair in love and water.**

4. **An apple a day keeps the greengrocer busy.**

5. **The proof of the pudding is in the heating.**

6. **Look before you sneeze.**

7. One swallow does not make a hiccup.

8. Let sleeping dogs slobber.

9. A friend in need is a nuisance.

10. A bird in the hand is worth two in the bathroom.

11. Rome was not built in a cupboard.

12. Don't count your chickens before they're microwaved.

13. The hand that rocks the cradle rules the waves.

14. Don't try to run before you can burp.

15. Half a loaf is better than cabbage.

Too much thinking makes my head hurt!

Answers
1. The early bird catches the worm.
2. Don't put all your eggs into one basket.
3. All's fair in love and war.
4. An apple a day keeps the doctor away.
5. the proof of the pudding is in the eating.
6. Look before you leap.
7. One swallow does not make a summer.
8. Let sleeping dogs lie.
9. A friend in need is a friend indeed.
10. A bird in the hand is worth two in the bush.
11. Rome was not built in a day.
12. Don't count your chickens before they're hatched.
13. The hand that rocks the cradle rules the world.
14. Don't try to run before you can walk.
15. Half a loaf is better than none.

Teacher "Who was the first woman in the world, Jennifer?"

Jennifer "Don't know, miss!"

Teacher "I'll give you a clue - think of apples!"

Jennifer "Granny Smith, miss!"

Teacher "You're late for school again Peter!"

Peter "Sorry, miss! I sprained my ankle!?"

Teacher "Huh! that's a lame excuse!"

Teacher "Susan, give me a sentence containing the word "gruesome'!"

Susan "My Dad bought a greenhouse and gruesome tomatoes!?"

Teacher "Who was Ivanhoe, Mandy?"

Mandy "A Russian gardener, miss?"

Teacher "Who can tell me when the Forth Bridge was built?"

David "I know, sir! When the third one fell down!"

Teacher "What was King Arthur's court famous for, Darren?"

Darren "It's Knight life, sir!"

Teacher "We have a new boy in class. Where are you from, Ivor?"

Ivor "Wales, sir?"

Teacher "What part?"

Ivor "All of me, sir!"

Teacher "What was King Arthur's court famous for, Darren?"

Darren "It's Knight life, sir!"

Teacher "Patrick, give me a sentence containing the word 'centimetre'."

Patrick "Easy, sir! When my Granny came over from Ireland, I was centimetre!"

Teacher "Point to America on the map for me, Charles."

Charles "It's there, miss!"

Teacher "Now can you tell me who discovered America?"

Linda "Charles, miss!"

You Just Need Plain Paper to make . . .
The World's Best
PAPER PLANE!

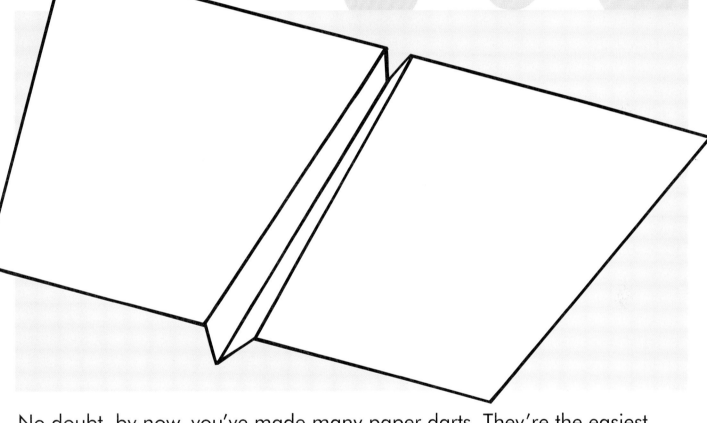

No doubt, by now, you've made many paper darts. They're the easiest paper plane to make and to fly. But they don't hold a candle to this little beauty which glides like a seagull on an up-current and seems to fly on and on … and on!

Here's a step-by-step guide how to make it …

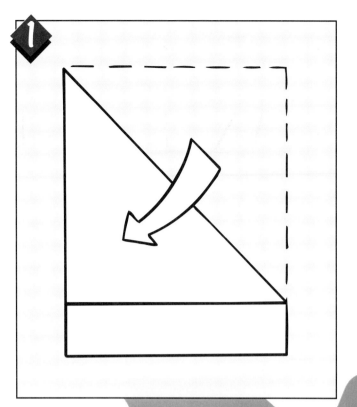

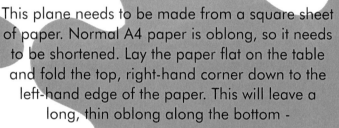

This plane needs to be made from a square sheet of paper. Normal A4 paper is oblong, so it needs to be shortened. Lay the paper flat on the table and fold the top, right-hand corner down to the left-hand edge of the paper. This will leave a long, thin oblong along the bottom -

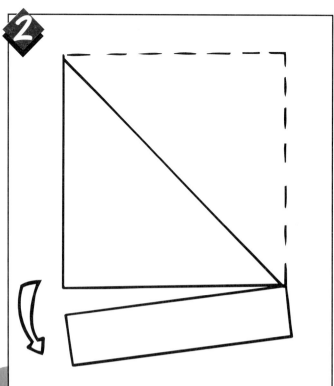

Fold along the edge of the bottom oblong several times so that the paper will tear or use a pair of scissors to cut off this piece. Your piece of paper is now square -

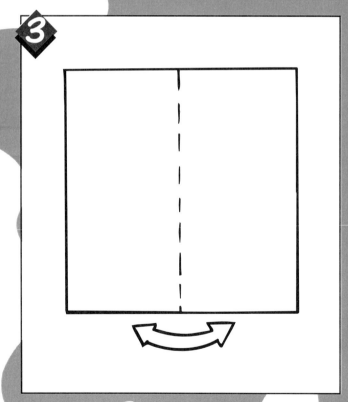

Smooth out your newly-formed square and fold it in half down the middle -

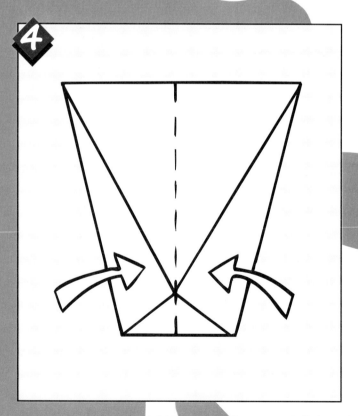

This is the first tricky bit! Take the bottom, left-hand corner and fold it over so that it just touches the middle crease. Then do the same with the bottom right-hand corner. When you have finished, the two corners will just touch in the centre like this -

5

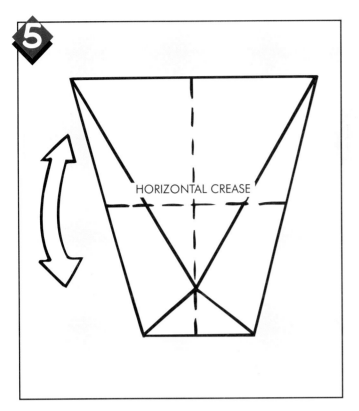

HORIZONTAL CREASE

Fold the thinner bottom edge of the aeroplane
up to the wider top edge …
and then unfold it again.
This will give you a central,
horizontal crease -

6

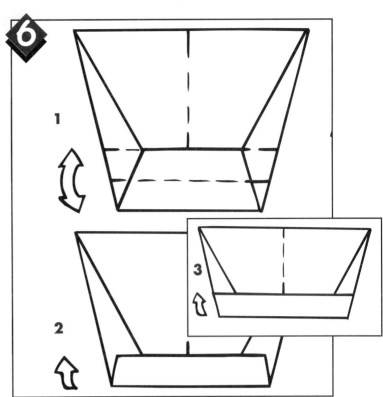

1

2

3

Now for the **second** tricky bit! You have to fold the
bottom edge THREE TIMES to make the weighted
nose of the plane.

FIRST FOLD   bottom edge right up to the central
crease you made in the previous step.
This gives you a double thickness.

SECOND FOLD   new bottom edge to central crease.
This gives you treble thickness.

THIRD FOLD   triple thick section back OVER central
crease. This makes the heavy nose longer.

7

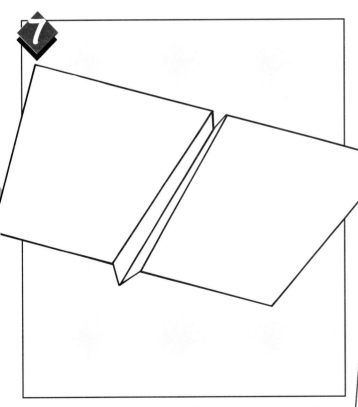

Fold your plane in half down the central,
vertical crease. Then, leaving just a narrow
fuselage, fold down the wings on either side so
that your finished plane looks like this -

FINAL TIPS AND SUGGESTIONS

Your plane should glide well from the start. This is
because all the folding has given it a weighted nose.
But if it stalls when you throw it (ie, flies upwards, stops
and falls backwards), the nose is still not heavy enough.
Either fold it again or, better still, add a paper clip.

Another way to make your plane glide better is to
gently bend the back corners of the wings upwards.

Your plane can be made to look as exciting as it flies by
colouring it with felt tips (the brighter the better!)

If you make these aeroplanes with a whole group of
Cub Scout friends, you can hold gliding competitions to
see whose plane can stay in the air the longest or fly the
greatest distance. It's great fun … and you're learning
the science of flight all the time!

'WHEN'-SDAY

'THIRST'-DAY

Baby Drivers

This is what I call a Big Boy's Toy!

Shh! Don't tell Mum where we got the pram wheels!

Er, I've just realised this thing doesn't have brakes!

Is it me, or does that front wheel look a bit wonky?

Photograph: Peter Owen

Glorious Food . . .

Just coming up for air!

Can swallow this in one piece!

Photograph: M Trayhorn

Is this sausage ever going to cook?

Photograph: M. Trayhorn

I thought this divining-rod was supposed to lead to water!

Photograph: Chalfont

Portrait Gallery

Photograph: Chris Boardman

Photograph: David Garton

Photograph: Dave Wood

CHEESE!

Photograph: Ron Crabb

Photograph: Stan White

Photograph: Chris Boardman

Photograph: Ron Crabb

Messing about on the River

Do I look cool or what!

Photograph: Chris Boardman

Tell that duck to stop nibbling my toes!

Photograph: David Garton

Oh, 'water' laugh this is!

Photograph: Richard Bridgeman

Hey, look down there – a d-d-dorsal fin!

Meet a master cartoonist and learn how to gain your Artist Badge ...

SCOUTMASTER SNOOPY

A beagle in his time plays many parts - and one of them is the leader of a very small (but still unruly) Scout Troop. Like Scout Leaders all over the world, Scoutmaster Snoopy exercises enormous patience as he takes his "troops" trekking through the countryside. And the Scouts themselves (Woodstock and his other feathered friends) exhibit a similar mixture of enthusiasm, obedience and fear!

Here's a brief glimpse into the wonderful world of Snoopy, Charlie Brown, Peanuts and the strip's creator, Charles Schulz - followed by some ideas about how you can gain your Artist Badge by cartooning ...

THE SNOOPY FACT FILE

Snoopy is without doubt the most famous cartoon dog of all time. The image of him lying on top of his doghouse is known all round the world.

The beagle superstar never speaks - that would be one human trait too many - but he manages to convey every emotion by facial expression and thought balloons.

Snoopy has a vivid imagination and has created a number of different personalities for himself in addition to being a Scoutmaster (or, more correctly, a Beagle Scout). These include 'Joe Cool'; the 'World War 1 Flying Ace' who chases his sworn enemy, The Red Baron; the 'Literary Ace' working on his new novel which always begins: "It was a dark and stormy night …" and many, many others.

Chocolate chip cookies are Snoopy's passion, closely followed by pepperoni pizza and ginger beer!

PEANUTS

Snoopy belongs to Charlie Brown and refers to his master as: "that round-headed kid". Named after a real person (one of the cartoonist's friends), Charlie Brown is just as famous as his four-legged companion. He is the loser with whom everyone can identify. Everything goes wrong for "good ol' Charlie Brown" - his kite always gets stuck up a tree, he never manages to kick his American football or win a game of baseball, and he never succeeds in going out with the love of his life, the little red-haired girl.

Charlie Brown and Snoopy appear in Peanuts, a phenomenally successful cartoon strip that appears in over 2000 different newspapers in over 60 countries every day! From Monday to Saturday, it is a short, three-frame strip; on a Sunday, it is a longer, seven or eight frame strip. And, at one time or another, it has been translated into 26 languages - including Latin!

The very first Peanuts strip was published on October 2nd, 1950. That means it has been appearing every single day (without repeats) for a staggering 49 years! And it's all been the work of one man, a modest and mild-mannered cartoonist known since his childhood as 'SPARKY'.

CHARLES SCHULZ

Sparky Schulz was born on November 26th, 1922 in Minneapolis, a city in Minnesota, USA. His father, Carl Schulz, was a hard-working barber with two passions, fishing and newspaper comic strips. Initially, his son shared his passions, but eventually Charles Schulz gave up fishing because, as he said:

"Those fish are having a good time down there."
The love of newspaper cartoons, however, remained.

Schulz was brilliant at drawing from an early age and his pre-school teacher predicted that he would become an artist. As a young man, he studied cartooning on a correspondence course, then became an instructor with the school, and finally established himself as a cartoonist himself.

Peanuts was a success almost right from the start. Snoopy and his friends have appeared on countless licensed products, from tee-shirts to toothbrushes, and have appeared in 30 TV specials and four feature films. Paperback collections of the strips have sold well over 300 million copies!

INK AND THINK BALLOONS!

How To Gain Your Artist Badge

Inventing your own cartoon character and drawing your own cartoon strip will fit requirements 2a and also 2g. And what could impress your examiner more than an original cartoon full of funny incidents and bright colours!

Here's the official list of requirements for gaining this Badge...

1. Know the primary colours and demonstrate how to mix paints to make other colours.
2. Choose three other activities from the list below. One of these activities is to be done in the presence of the examiner:

a Draw with pencil, brush, pen or crayon an original illustration of any imaginary incident, character or scene.

b Design and make a greetings card.

c Make a poster advertising Cub Scouting or a Cub Scout event.

d Make a design and print in on paper or fabric, eg, using potato or lino cuts.

e Design and make a decorated book cover.

f Draw or paint a picture from observation.

g Complete any other suitable activity agreed with the examiner.

Here are some helpful hints to get you started...

- Make it easy for yourself - invent a character who is simple to draw. Remember, your character must look more or less the same in every frame of the strip.

- You might find it easier to invent two characters who are in conflict with one another. There can be more scope for storylines and fun that way.

- Don't be afraid to experiment with sketches before you actually start drawing your strip. Remember the writer and artist's motto: "When in doubt - waste paper!"

- Make the first frame of your story the Title Frame. Print the name of your character and maybe the title of your story.

- Leave plenty of room in each frame of your story for Speech Balloons. Don't put too many words in them - and keep them horizontal (ie, reading in straight lines from left to right.) Print the words in capital letters if you can.

- Try to put some funny incidents in your story - comic accidents, people falling over or bumping into one another etc. This makes for funny reading.

- Use lots of Sound Effects to tell your reader what is happening. Write words like Splat! Splash! Thud! Blam! Biff! Etc on your pictures in big letters.

- Be very careful how you colour your finished story. Felt pens are best. If you colour in the backgrounds, do it very lightly in pencil crayon only. It is very easy to "swamp" your pictures and make them difficult to read.

- At the very end, you might like to go round the outlines of your main characters with a thin, black pen. This "picks out" the important parts of each frame and tells your reader where to look.

- If you want to do a really professional job, write a script first and draw from that. You can use a computer for scripting and it may help you to avoid going wrong half-way through the drawing and having to start all over again.

On the page opposite is a layout grid to photocopy for your picture strip story. It will work best if you enlarge it to A3 size.

Super Six Puzzle Parade

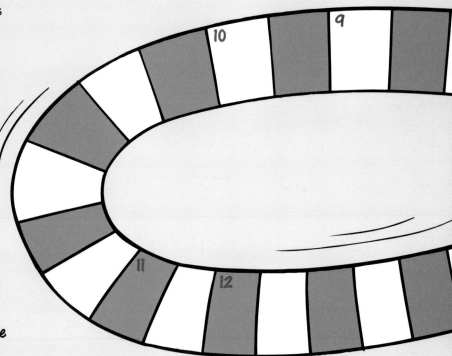

Young Sammy is wild about animals and, through his Cub Scout Pack, does everything he can to help them - especially those species that are in danger.

To find his favourite animals, solve the clues and write your answers into the snake. Remember, the last letter of each name is also the first letter of the next name. Then, when you have done all 20, can you pick out the animal that is the most endangered in the wild?

Clues

1. African big cat. Fastest runner in the world. Never play cards with them!
2. African wild dog. Scavenges in packs. Noted for "laughing"!
3. Eats ants!
4. Lives in Arctic Circle. Big antlers. Associated with Father Christmas.
5. Large rodent. Most people hate them. Live in sewers and spread disease.
6. Big cat from India. Striped. Lives alone and inhabits ruined buildings.
7. Male goat.
8. Lives in trees. Often intelligent. Our early ancestor.
9. Huge ox from Tibet. Long, shaggy coat. Name is slang for talking too much!
10. Australian animal. Bounds about. Keeps young in a pouch.
11. Bird of prey. Supposed to be wise. "Twit-twoo"!
12. Another big cat. This one famous for its spots. Often lies in trees.
13. Goes "quack"!
14. Cute-looking Australian animal. Wrongly called a bear. Eats eucalyptus leaves.
15. Deer of the open plains. Tall, pointed horns. Runs very fast.
16. Has a trunk and never forgets!
17. Found in ponds in Spring. Grows into a frog.
18. Huge bird of prey. Very fierce with amazing eyesight. Symbol of the Roman Army and national emblem of America.
19. Female Sheep.
20. Flightless Australian bird. Aggressive - especially when with Rod Hull!

WORDSNAKE

OF ALL THESE ANIMALS, THE ONE MOST IN DANGER OF EXTINCTION IS THE TIGER.

I borrowed this book from Brenda. If I don't give it back, I'll be in danger of extinction!

CHEETAHYENANTEATEREINDEERATIGERAMONKEYAKANGAROOWLEOPARDUCKOA LANTELOPELEPHANTADPOLEAGLEWEMU

(Here are the answers run together with overlapping letters, but they are not in the final form of the snake)

ANSWERS: 1.Cheetah 2.Hyena 3.Anteater 4.Reindeer 5.Rat 6.Tiger 7.Ram 8.Monkey 9.Yak 10.Kangaroo 11.Owl 12.Leopard 13.Duck 14.Koala 15.Antelope 16.Elephant 17.Tadpole 18.Eagle 19.Ewe 20.Emu

The Old Jokes Home

What do kangaroos eat in Chinese restaurants?

Hop Suey!

What's the sweetest rhythm of all?

Sugar Beat!

What's white and speeds down the aisle going "choo, choo!"?

A bridal train!

What's the best present you can give a man who has everything?

Anti-biotics

What can give you an injection at 100 mph?

An e-type jab!

What's the difference between Santa Claus and a hot dog?

Santa wears a red suit - the dog just pants!

What do you call an alarm clock that won't go off?

A false-alarm clock!

Which famous film star jumps over trees?

John Tree-vaulter!

What do you call a Judge who's only 3 feet tall?

A small thing sent to try us!

What are the longest words in the English language?

Post Office - they always have millions of letters!

We Do Like SNAKES!

A Beginner's Guide To Keeping (Non-Poisonous) SNAKES

Unlike tarantulas, snakes are not so delicate and, once tame, can be taken out and handled - making them exciting, interactive pets. But, like the big spiders, they are essentially tropical animals which need to be kept warm and properly fed to stay healthy. And they are shy, sensitive creatures with special requirements of their own.

Here's what you need to know if you're thinking of keeping one ...

THE VIVARIUM

Obviously, the size of the cage you need depends on the size of your snake. Proper, wooden-framed, glass-fronted cases are best, but they are expensive to buy. Small snakes live perfectly well in glass aquariums designed for fish and these are much cheaper.

Don't put sand or peat inside your cage as the snake tends to swallow the find particles. Wood-bark chippings can be used, but there is a danger that they can carry small mites. The best thing with which to line your tank is actually newspaper - it is cheap, easy to change and warm for the snake. Snakes also like cardboard boxes with holes in them to hide in. And they must have water at all times. Use a heavy china dish rather than a plastic one so that the snake can't knock it over.

HEATING AND LIGHTING

Your pet snake must be kept warm at all times. During the day, a light can be kept on using a normal bulb and electric socked from any DIY store or electrical shop. The amount of heat generated by the light depends on the size of the bulb. Monitor this with a simple cage thermometer on the outside of the glass. These are easily obtained from pet shops and are very cheap.

At night, when you don't want the light on but your snake still needs to be warm, use a heat-pad. These are also available from pet shops and cost about £15. This is an essential item for which you need to budget when getting a pet snake. On a cold night, a heat-pad is literally a matter of life and death for your pet!

FEEDING

Most captive snakes eat mice and small rats. In this country, it is illegal to put live prey into a snake's tank. Equally importantly, it is dangerous for the snake - when cornered, these fierce little rodents will fight back! So buy frozen ones from the pet shop and thaw them out at room temperature for several hours before putting them into the cage. Your hungry snake should find them immediately and swallow them whole.

SHEDDING

You should not attempt to feed your snake if he is about to shed his skin. You'll know that this is about to happen because his eyes will go "milky" looking. Shedding can take several days and healthy snakes should have no trouble losing their old skin themselves. You might find that recently-moved snakes, or old ones, run into difficulties and leave bits of skin behind. These must be removed because they can cause irritations and infections. The best way is to put your snake into a bag of wet moss for a couple of hours. This will make the skin soft and you should be able to peel it off. If not, go to the vet!

BEGINNER-FRIENDLY SPECIES

The following breeds are the popular ones for a young snake-keeper!

Corn Snake   (Elaphe guttata)
Grass Snake (Natrix natrix)
Garter Snake (Thamnophis)
and
King Snake   (Lampropeltis)

THE SNAKE

✦ All snakes are carnivorous (eat other animals).

✦ Snakes are reptiles, closely related to lizards.

✦ There are about 2,700 different species of snake, living everywhere in the world except on mountain tops and the North and South Poles.

✦ Snakes are cold-blooded and rely on outside heat to raise their body temperature and make them function.

✦ The majority of snakes are harmless; a few carry deadly poison.

✦ Snakes range in size from just a few cm (like a worm) to the gigantic Reticulated Python of Asia.

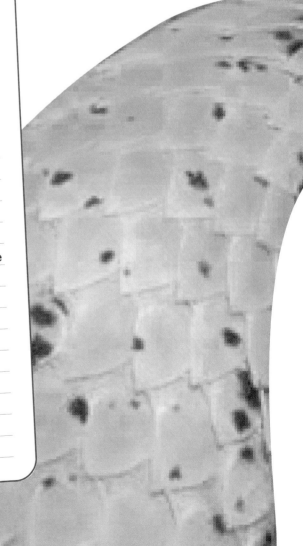

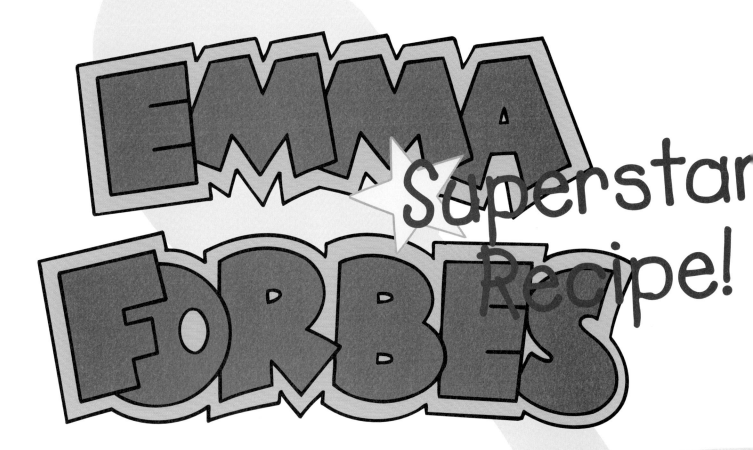

EMMA FORBES

★Superstar Recipe!

Chocolate Chip Cookies

A couple of years ago, Scouting Magazine asked a number of famous show-biz personalities to donate their favourite recipe which would be published in a fund-raising book for charity.

Some of these are suitable for Cub Scouts to make - provided you heed the warning below. Let's start with this one ...

If you would like more celebrity recipes like this one, then the book 'TOP NOSH' is just for you. Telephone the Scout Information Centre on 0845 300 1818 for details.

WHAT YOU DO -

1 Pre-heat the oven to 180(C / Gas Mark 4.

2 Put the butter and both types of sugar into the bowl. Add the egg and vanilla essence and beat together with the wooden spoon. The finished mixture should be light and fluffy.

3 Add the flour and milk. Stir in and beat together again.

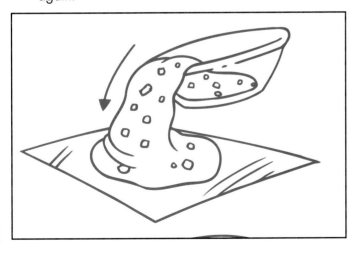

4 Stir in the chocolate chips. Then wrap the mixture in greaseproof paper and leave in the fridge for about 15 minutes.

WHAT YOU NEED

- A mixing bowl
- Wooden spoon
- Milk Jug
- Greaseproof paper
- Two baking trays
- Wire cooling rack
- 170g butter
- 113g caster sugar
- 57g dark, soft, brown sugar
- 1 egg
- Half a teaspoon of vanilla essence
- 227g self-raising flour
- 2 tablespoons of milk
- 2 bags of ready-made chocolate chips (about) 17g)

5 Unwrap the chilled mixture and break off small amounts with a teaspoon. Rub a little butter onto your baking tray to grease them and then place the mounds of mixture all over them. (They need to be well spaced because the biscuits spread whilst they are cooking.)

6 Bake for about 12 to 15 minutes, until golden brown. Place on the wire rack and cool before eating.

WARNING Take great care when lighting and using the oven. Make sure a grown-up is on hand and knows what you are doing. Cooking can be dangerous - never try it on your own.

CORNFLAKES FROM JOHN CLEESE

WHAT YOU NEED -
Bowl   Spoon   Cornflakes   Milk

WHAT YOU DO -
Buy a packet of cornflakes.

Open the cardboard box.

Open the sort-of-plastic pocked inside the box.

Pour the contents (sort of yellowy-brownish bits of things) onto a plate.

Buy a bottle of milk.

Take the top off the thin end of the bottle.

Invert the bottle gently over the cornflakes, making sure that the milk does not go all over the edge of the plate.

It's very simple to make and absolutely delicious.
An alternative is to use cola instead of milk.
Add basil as required.

Serves one person.

Beans On Toast from Rowan Atkinson (Mr Bean)

WHAT YOU NEED -
Saucepan   Toaster   Tin of baked beans
Sliced bread

WHAT YOU DO -
Make the toast.

Heat the beans in the saucepan until they go all bubbly.

Pour over the toast and eat.
Serves one person.

THE ADVENTURE CREST AWARD

Quiz Time

Here's a fun quiz based on the highest award you can win as a Cub Scout -
the Adventure Crest Award. There are four sections from within the award,
with ten general knowledge questions about each. See how well you get on ...

SPORTS AND HOBBIES

1. **Which game is played with a shuttlecock?**

   Squash   Badminton   Tiddly Winks

2. **If you were a 'twitcher', what would your hobby be?**

   Watching horror films   Helping nervous people
   Bird watching

3. **The game of rugby is named after Rugby School where it was first played.**

   True? False?

4. **Connect these top football teams to the grounds where they play -**

   Manchester United   White Hart Lane

   Chelsea   Old Trafford

   Tottenham Hotspur   Highbury

   Arsenal   Stamford Bridge

5. **Model aeroplanes that can fly have to be built from a special, lightweight wood. What is it called?**

   Oak   Balsa   Chipboard

6. **Can you complete this sentence -**

   'A philatelist is someone whose hobby is collecting

   _____.'

7. **What is a 'googly'?**

   A rare bird   A juicy, tropical fruit
   A type of spin-bowling used in cricket

8. **Haggis-rolling is a popular sport in the north of Scotland. It involves two teams of men wearing kilts chasing a haggis down a mountain slope.**

   True? False?

9. **What is a 'spinnaker'?**

   A special, high-speed top
   An extra sail used in yacht-racing
   A green vegetable eaten by Popeye

10. **What kind of game is 'whist'?**

    A card game   A board game   A ball game

ANSWERS 1. Badminton 2. Bird watching 3. true
4. Manchester United - Old Trafford   Chelsea - Stamford Bridge
Tottenham Hotspur - White Hart Lane   Arsenal - Highbury
5. Balsa 6. Stamps 7. A type of spin-bowling used in cricket
8. False 9. An extra sail used in yachtracing
10. A card game

SCIENCE AND NATURE

1. The hoopoe is a beautifully coloured bird with a feathered crest that occasionally visits the south of England.

   True? False?

2. Which famous scientist is supposed to have discovered the Law Of Gravity when an apple fell on his head?

   William Tell   Sir Isaac Newton   Adam

3. Which one of these big cats is known to like swimming in water -

   Lion   Tiger   Jaguar   Puma

4. What is a 'pipette'?

   A glass instrument used for measuring liquids

   A type of bat   A type of grape

5. Where would you find The Sea Of Tranquility?

   Blackpool   Inside the Earth   On The Moon

6. Where does a rattlesnake keep his rattle?

   At the end of his tail   Behind his venom fangs
   Under his bed with his dummy

7. What scale is used to measure the strength of earthquakes?

   The Beauford Scale   The Richter Scale   The Piano Scale

8. During the mating season, male swordfish fight duels with each other using their long, pointed noses like swords.

   True?   False?

9. 'Au' is the chemical symbol for which precious commodity?

   Gold   Silver   Diamonds   Pearls
   A Cup Final ticket

10. What is a Portuguese Man-O-War?

    A jellyfish with a nasty sting   An old galleon
    A holidaymaker from Portugal whose ice-cream has just been knocked out of his hand by your football.

ANSWERS   1. True   2. Sir Isaac Newton   3. Tiger
4. A glass instrument for measuring liquids   5. On The Moon
6. At the end of his tail   7. The Richter Scale   8. False
9. Gold   10. A jellyfish with a nasty sting

78

CREATIVITY

1. William Shakespeare is generally regarded as the greatest writer in the English language. Where was he born?

   Milton Keynes   London   Stratford-upon-Avon

2. Which famous puppet found his nose grew longer and longer when he told a lie?

   Mr Punch   Pinocchio   Sooty

3. Desperate Dan is the star of the UK's best-selling comic, The Beano.

   True?   False?

4. Which well-known composer went deaf in later life and was unable to hear the beautiful music he had written?

   Beethoven   Mozart   Mustapha Eartrumpet

5. Who wrote 'Oliver Twist' and many other long novels set in Victorian London?

   Enid Blyton   Jane Austen   Charles Dickens

6. Unscramble these letters to find the name of the sailor who was cast away on a desert island in a famous story by Daniel Defoe -

   N S O R B N I O   R S U E O C

7. Can you complete the names of the four Beatles -

   John _____

   _____ McCartney

   Ringo _____

   _____ Harrison

8. The Mona Lisa is probably the most famous painting in the world. Who painted it?

   Vincent Van Gough   Leonardo da Vinci
   Rolf Harris

9. What is the difference between a biography and an autobiography? (Answer in your own words)

   _____

   _____

   _____

10. If you performed a 'pas-de'deux', what sort of dance would you be doing?

    A war dance   A disco dance   A ballet dance

COUNTRIES AND CULTURE

1. What is the popular and incorrect name for the Inuit people of the Arctic Circle?

   Vikings   Eskimos   Snowmen

2. Can you complete this sentence -

   'The country, _____
   is famous for its tulips, windmills, clogs and cheese.'

3. From left to right, what colours are the French flag?

   Red, white and blue   Blue, white and red
   Red and yellow and pink and blue

4. If you went into a shop to spend some Yen, you would be visiting Japan.

   True?   False?

5. Which one of these is not a Native American tribe?

   The Apache   The Sioux   The Blackfoot
   The Smellyfoot   The Cherokee

6. If you visited the Taj Mahal in India, what would you see?

   A beautiful palace   A hotel
   A take-away restaurant

7.   This symbol is known as the Star of David -

   To which world religion does it belong?

   Buddhism   Hinduism   Judaism

8. Pizza, lasagne, spaghetti and other pasta dishes - now eaten throughout the world - were first cooked in Greece.

   True?   False?

9. In which country are you most likely to see men wearing their traditional costume of 'lederhosen' or leather trousers (usually shorts)?

   France   Germany   Russia

10. What is the name of the native people of Australia?

   Aborigines Maoris   Neighbours

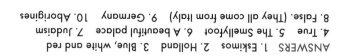

ANSWERS 1. Eskimos 2. Holland 3. Blue, white and red
4. True 5. The Smellyfoot 6. A beautiful palace 7. Judaism
8. False. (They all come from Italy) 9. Germany 10. Aborigines

80

What do you get if you cross a chicken with some cement?
A BRICKLAYER!

What do you get if you cross an owl that's lost its voice with a skunk?
A BIRD THAT SMELLS BUT DOESN'T GIVE A HOOT!

What do you get if you cross a sheepdog with a jelly?
THE COLLIEWOBBLES!

What do you get if you cross a gun dog with a telephone?
A GOLDEN RECEIVER!

What do you get if you cross a baby carriage with Shakespeare's Prince Of Denmark?
PRAMLET!

What do you get if you cross a bottle of cold lemonade with a cat?
A THIRST-AID KIT!

What do you get if you cross a snowman with a great white shark?
FROSTBITE!

What do you get if you cross a cat with an unripe lemon?
A SOURPUSS!

What do you get if you cross a sparrow's leg with a trout and a hand?
BIRDSTHIGH FISH FINGERS!

What do you get if you cross your brain with some elastic?
A STRETCH OF THE IMAGINATION!

Jane's Generation Gap Triple Puzzle

ARE YOU INTO POP MUSIC? Jane is - in a big way! Not only does she know all about current chart-toppers, she also digs her Mum's music of the 1980s and her Granny's music of the 1960s!

Find out Jane's favourite singers from three generations by solving this puzzle.
Below you'll find five simple clues. Solve them and write your answers into the grid.
Then you'll find that each letter in the grid has a reference letter and number (A1, B3, C5 etc).
Using these references, work out the names on the page opposite.

WHICH ONE DO YOU LIKE BEST?

	A	B	C	D	E
1					
2					
3					
4					
5					

1. Hammerheads, tigers and great whites are types of these

2. Person who flies an aircraft

3. Wooden seat found in the park

4. Smothered in jam - or very lucky!

5. Another name for a sentry

Jane's generation -

E2	B1	B3

A1	A2	B2	D3	B3

A5	B2	D1	C2	A1

Jane's Mum's generation -

C4	B2	D3	E3	C1	B3	C2

A4	C1	D3	E1	A1	D2	C3

Jane's Granny's generation -

E2	B1	B3

A3	B3	C1	E2	C2	B3	A1

The Super Six in
"Sammy's Good Turn"

Sammy was close to gaining his Cub Scout Award. He had completed all the other parts, including learning about first aid and about his Promise, and now all he had to do was some Good Turns.

"I'll help the others with whatever they're doing!" cried Sammy, jumping onto his little bike and speeding round to the Pack Meeting.

At the Scout Hut, Jane was busy working for her Craftsman Badge. She was good at sewing and had made herself a cute, red mini-dress.

"I can wear this to the Fun Fair tonight," she chuckles, going outside to admire her handiwork in the daylight.

Next moment, Sammy arrived.

"Hi, Jane!" he called. "Anything I can do to help you ... ooops!"

The little Cub Scout had skidded to a halt in a puddle, sending a shower of mud all down Jane's' new dress!

"Yes, there is something you can do to help me, Sammy," hissed Jane. "GO AWAY!"

Jane went back into the hut to wash her dress, so Sammy went in search of the others. Akela told him that Joe and Ice were round the back of the Scout hut, but when he arrived his two friends were not there. Instead, he found a big tent spread out on the ground with all the awnings and groundsheets arranged beside it.

"I bet they're checking their equipment for the Camper Badge," exclaimed Sammy, excitedly. "I could help them b y packing it all up again!"

Sammy set to work, folding the canvas from side to side and pressing all the air out of it as he went. It was a terrible struggle to get everything to fit into the tent bag, but at last he managed it.

"There!" he puffed, painting proudly at the packed tent just as Joe and Ice came round the corner.

"What have you done?" howled Joe.

"P-p-packed your tent up for you ..." stammered Sammy.

"This is not cool, little man!" sighed Ice. "Out tent was wet. We wanted it left out in the air to dry!"

"Boobed again!" groaned Sammy.

Leaving Joe and Ice to unpack their tent once more, Sammy hurried off to find Gus and Brenda.

"I must be able to help them!" he said.

The pair were in the cookery area. Gus, who was very fond of food, was trying to gain his Cook Badge and Brenda had offered to help him. Despite eating a lot of the mixture with his fingers, Gus had succeeded in baking a beautiful cake. Brenda had shown him how to ice it and now he was on his way to show Akela, who was acting as examiner for this award.

Suddenly, Sammy burst in.

"Hi, guys!" he cried. "I've come to ..."

This time, he did not get as far as the "ooops!"

The door he had thrown open knocked the cake right out of Gus's hand. It flew through the air and landed with a splat! in Brenda's face!

"I've had enough of this!" yelled Sammy.

"You've had enough of this ..." spluttered Brenda.

Sammy decided to give up his idea of doing good turns to the other members of his Six. Having said sorry to all of them, he jumped on his bike again and set off for home.

On the way, he passed the Fun Fair which was just coming to life for the evening's business. In the gutter, about to tall down the drain, lay a bunch of keys. Sammy skidded to a halt again and rescued the keys.

"These could belong to anybody," he thought to himself. "I'd better take them down to the Police Station."

When he arrived at the Lost Property desk, an elderly man in an old overcoat was already there. His eyes lit up when he saw what Sammy was handing to the Sergeant.

"My keys!" he whooped. "Thank goodness you've found them!"

The old man was from the Fun Fair. He owned the Carousel.

"Without these keys, sonny jim," he chuckled, "I wouldn't have been able to get my roundabout started this evening."

As a special reward for handing in the lost keys, the Carousel owner gave free rides to Sammy and his friends. Of course, Sammy fetched the other members of his Six to join him at the fair. Soon, Gus and the other four were all sitting with Sammy, going round and round and up and down on the colourful, painted horses.

"We're glad you managed to do a good turn after all, Sammy," laughed Jane.

"Yeah!" agreed Sammy, "and this Carousel is the best "GOOD TURN" of all!"

Fun in the Sun

How did I get roped in for this?

Photograph: Peter Owen

And I thought Golf was a Volkswagen!

Photograph: Ron Crobb

Phew! This is mighty 'tyre'-ing!

Photograph: Richard Brideman

Now I know what they mean by 'around the pole'

Photograph: Peter Owen

All Dressed Up

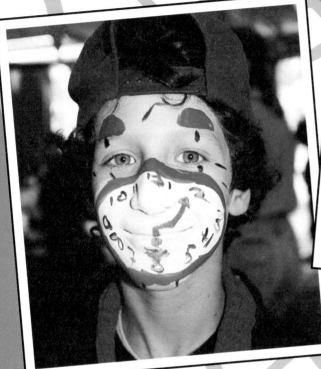

I've had the "time" of my life!

Photograph: Chris Boardman

Just clowning around!

Photograph: D.A. Davis

We are Star dust, we are golden...

Punk is alive and well and living at summer camp

Photograph: Jane Ainley

and somewhere to go!

At the End Of The Day...

Now where did I put that kitchen sink?

Photograph: Schofield-Smith

Never stand when you can sit and never sit when you can SLEEP!

Photograph: Mark S. Gwynne

We're happy and we know it...

Is our tent cool or what?

Photograph: G. Rhodes

Special Activity Feature
Learn about a famous French painter and gain your Gardener Badge...

Monet Makes
The World Go Round!

1999 was Claude Monet's year. An exhibition of his later paintings at the Royal Academy Of Arts in London was a runaway success, proving what everyone already knew - that Monet is one of the most popular painters of all time.

Here's the story of his life, and of the garden he made at Giverny which is almost as famous as he is ...

MAKING THE RIGHT IMPRESSION

Up until about 1860, the main trend in painting was Realism. In other words, artists painted pictures which looked real and their skill was judged on how accurate their paintings looked. Claude Monet changed all that. With the help of some fellow artists, he introduced a new idea. Instead of painting a scene accurately, he painted the impression of the scene - the shapes, the colours and, above all, the light. This meant that Monet could convey how the scene made you feel, rather than just what it looked like. This style of painting came to be known as 'Impressionism' and Monet was the undoubted inventor and leader of the movement.

EARLY DAYS

Claude Monet was born on November 14th, 1840, in Paris. His father, who was a grocer, soon moved to Le Havre, the French channel port opposite Portsmouth. Here, in his childhood, Monet watched the passing ships and noted the ever-changing weather and light of the seaside. He was obviously a talented artist, drawing beautiful pictures of ships and selling his first sketch at the age of 15. But his painting career really took off when he met a fellow artist called Boudin who introduced him to painting oil pictures in the open air. This had not been done very often before and it set the young Monet off on a 60-year quest to capture the different moods of Nature and light on canvas.

Claude Monet's *The Water Lily Pond, 1900*

FAMOUS FRIENDS

In 1859, at the age of 19, Monet moved back to Paris. In true rebellious student fashion, he refused to attend the art school his parents wanted and, instead, hung around with a group of modern artists with whom he shared his ideas. These included Pissarro, Renoir and Sisley - all of whom were household names today. Renoir came to be his closest ally and, during the 1860s, the two artists went painting together, capturing the feel of the bathers and the rowing boats on the River Seine at a summer resort called La Grenouillere. These are some of the best-known Impressionist paintings in the world.

TAKE ONE ... AND TWO ... AND THREE ...

Monet continued to paint continuously throughout the 1870s and 80s. Travelling to England, Holland and around France, he painted picture after picture in his own special style. Then he developed the idea of painting the same scene over and over again at different times of day and in different weather. These series allowed Monet to explore how the changes in light changed how the scene looked and felt.

EVERYTHING IN THE GARDEN

In 1883, Monet settled in Giverny, a small village about 50 miles from Paris on the River Epte, a tributary of the Seine. This farmhouse, surrounded by an orchard, was to be his home until his death in December, 1926.

At first, Monet grew flowers in his garden and painted them. Then, in 1890, he bought a piece of marshland across the road from his house and, by diverting a local stream, created a water-garden. This lush place became the home of huge water-lilies, weeping willows and colourful irises. The garden was a work of art in itself, but it also gave Monet the perfect subject for painting. He devoted his later years to painting some huge canvases of this beautiful water garden - and it was these that proved so breathtaking at the exhibition at the Royal Academy earlier this year. Thanks to these fantastic paintings, Monet's garden has become known around the world and is now kept as a French National Monument.

THE FINAL TRIPS

In addition to painting his wonderful water-garden, Monet made two trips abroad in his later life, searching for new subjects to convey on canvas. He visited London on several occasions and painted a series of pictures of the River Thames, its bridges and the buildings of London. He also went to Venice in Italy, painting many of the canals and palaces there. Venice was a perfect subject for Impressionism - the light and reflection of the water and the magnificent old buildings made for colourful scenes that changed in appearance and feel almost by the minute!

In 1927, a year after Monet's death, two enormous oval rooms containing his water-garden pictures were dedicated to the artist at the Orangerie of the Tuileries Gallery in Paris. A later artist, likening the place to the great work of Michaelangelo, called it: "The Sistine Chapel Of Impressionism."

Information and illustrations kindly supplied by the Royal Academy Of Arts, London.

AND NOW IT'S OVER TO YOU ...

Toil And Soil!

HOW TO GAIN YOUR GARDENER BADGE

Here's the official list of requirements for gaining this badge ...

EITHER:

Look after a patch of garden, know what tools are needed and how to use and look after them. Grow something in your garden suitable for the time of year.

Or:

Grow a variety of plants indoors and know the conditions under which they must be kept.

CHOOSE ANY TWO OF THE FOLLOWING:

Grow vegetables or flowers from seed; know how to prick out and transplant.

Know about hazards to plants and flowers (eg, diseases, pests) and understand what preventative methods can be taken and what can be done to aid growth.

Know how to store vegetables and how long they may be stored.

Show how to prepare flowers for display.

Make a compost heap.

Carry out a soil test using a standard kit.

Help plan and plant a rockery garden, a fern or herb garden, herbacious border,
hanging basket, garden tub, etc.

Help maintain a lawn and

understand why it needs constant attention.

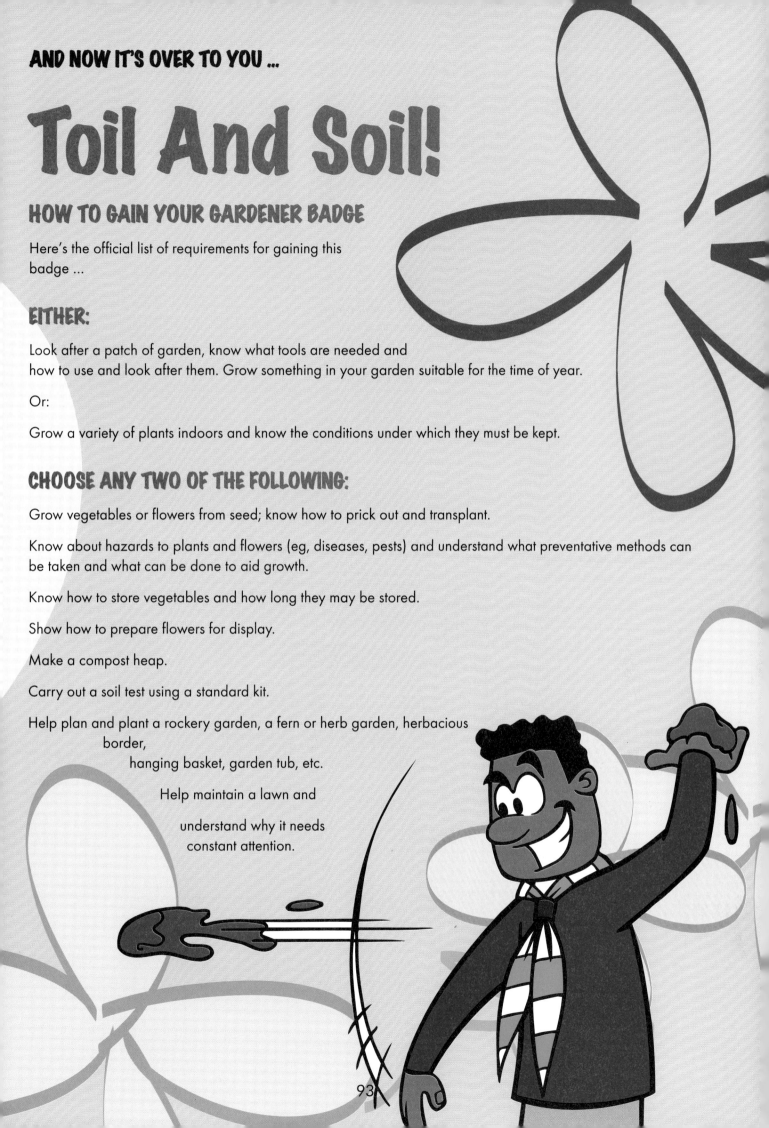

You will probably have your own ideas about how to gain your Gardener Badge, but in case you get stuck, here are a few suggestions for exciting things to do ...

BUILD A MODEL GARDEN

You need to find a cardboard shoebox and cut away one of the longer sides, making a "three walled" garden. Find a garden picture from a magazine and stick it to the back wall. Then collect gravel, pebbles, moss, twigs and small stones to make a path or crazy paving, a lawn, little flowerbeds and miniature rockeries.

You'll find that your model garden will keep for some time if the flowers are changed from time to time and all the greenery is kept moist.

BOTTLE GARDEN

It's great fun growing a garden in a bottle! Many glass containers are suitable for making them, and if they have a lid they will need very little watering because the water is kept in.

Here are some helpful tips:

Use a paper cone to pour the compost into your bottle.
- ✦ Take great care when dropping stones onto the bottle base.
- ✦ When watering, wash the inside of the bottle at the same time by pouring your water against the side of the neck so it runs down the side.
- ✦ Ask you local shop or gardening centre for suitable sized plants.
- ✦ Remove anything that grows too large and keep removing any dead leaves and flowers.

94

TRAY GARDENS

First, you need to fill a seed tray with soil or potting compost. Then 'landscape' it by laying a path of stones or putting in a pond made from a margarine tub. Then you can plant some small flowers or plants - or even grow the sops of root vegetables such as carrots, parsnips or swedes. (These will need to be started off in a saucer of water until they sprout from the top.)

Your tray garden should look like this-

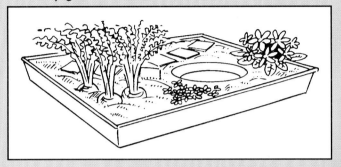

MORE ADVANCED MINIATURE GARDENS

Alternatively, you could try making one of these three -

Hanging Basket   **Garden In A Sink**   **Window Box**
                          (or a Sunken Garden)

THE REAL THING!

If you're lucky enough to have your own garden or can use the ground around your Scout Hut, there are literally a thousand and one things you can grow, depending on the time of year. You don't need lots of expensive tools, either. A spade, fork, rake, hoe, trowel and watering can are the main essentials.

When you're out in the garden, remember these simple rules -

✦ Make sure a grown-up knows what you are doing.
✦ Wear suitable clothes.
✦ Don't leave your tools lying around - put them away.
✦ Keep a constant eye on your garden. Weed and water regularly.

Now, like Monet, you've built your own garden, why not follow further in the great artist's footsteps and complete his most famous picture, using the colours below to guide you …

Claude Monet's The Water Lily Pond, 1900

JOE'S RIDDLE OF THE SANDS!

The Super Six are on a day trip to the seaside. They have all gone their separate ways - Sammy's playing crazy golf, Gus is at the candy floss stall, Jane's checking out the seafront boutiques, Brenda is beachcombing and Ice is sunning himself on the beach. But where's Joe?

When they get back to the minibus, the others find a note on the windscreen. In true Joe the joker fashion, it is all in riddles! Can you work out what the note says? Work out each letter from every two lines of the poems and write them in the spaces to the side. Then the five words, reading downwards, will tell you Joe's whereabouts!

Hi, guys! You'll find me at the . . .

My first is in apple
and also in tap;   _____

my second's in muddle,
in mug and in map;   _____

my third is in udder
and also in use;   _____

my fourth is in smoke
and is seen twice in shoes;   _____

my fifth is in egg,
but never in thumb;   _____

my sixth is in mice,
in maze and in mum; _____

my seventh is in elbow,
in Easter and prune; _____

my eighth is in neighbour
and also in noon; _____

my last is in tentpeg,
tennis and tune!

My first is in armchair,
in ace and in air; _____

my second's in rubble
and is seen twice in rare; _____

my third is cow
and also in cat; _____

my fourth's found in face,
in bat and in hat; _____

my fifth's twice in middle,
but never in wealth; _____

my last is in eagle
and also in elf!

My first is in John,
in Tom and in Ron; _____

my second's in long,
in lane and in gone.

My first is in tea,
in towel and in treat; _____

my second's in house
and also in heat; _____

my third comes in eel,
in end and in eat.

My first is in pipe
and also in pink; _____

my second's in India,
silly and ink; _____

my third is in trolley
and also in dear; _____

my last is in rat
and is seen twice in rear.

**They seek me here,
they seek me there ...**

The Old Jokes Home

I say, I say, I say!
What did the alarm clock's big hand say to the little hand?

"I'll be back in an hour!"

I say, I say, I say!
What did the flea on Robinson Crusoe's left knee say to the flea on his right knee?

"Cheerio! See you on Friday!"

I say, I say, I say!
What did the first lift say to the second lift?

"I think I'm going down with something!"

I say, I say, I say!
What did the mother crow say to the baby crow who was about to leave the nest?

"Listen, son - when you gotta crow, you gotta crow!"

I say, I say, I say!
What did the Baby Corn say to the Mummy Corn?

"Where's Pop corn?"

I say, I say, I say!
What did the left tonsil say to the right tonsil?

"Go and get dressed - the doctor's taking us out tonight!"

I say, I say, I say!
What did the boy magnet say to the girl magnet?

"I find you terribly attractive!"

I say, I say, I say!
What did the hedgehog say to the cactus?

"Hi, Dad!"

I say, I say, I say!
What did the first wall say to the second wall?

"Meet you at the corner!"

I say, I say, I say!
What did the toothpaste say to the toothbrush?

"Give me a quick squeeze and I'll meet you outside the tube!"

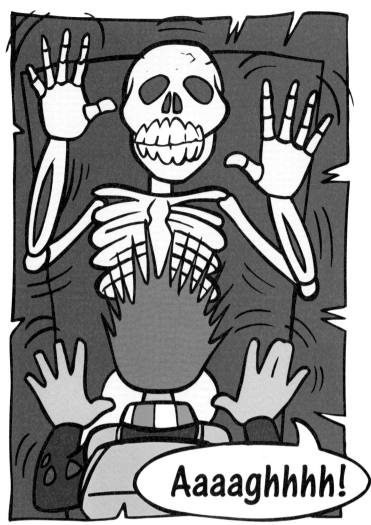

IN ANOTHER ROOM -

105

National Competition Report

'Water' Wonderful Show!

Say 'The Global Zone', 'The Green Land' or 'The Leisure Park' to someone in the street and they would probably think you were bonkers! Mention them to any Cub Scout, however, and they would know exactly what you were talking about! Why? Because these are some of the categories in "Waterwise", an exciting competition open to all UK Cub Scout Packs last year.

KNOWLEDGE, MONEY AND FUN!

"Waterwise" was organised by The Scout Association with the help of six Water Companies (Yorkshire, Northumbrian, Mid-Kent, South East and Mid Southern, Cambridge and Sutton & East Surrey) and various other organisations including the SeaLife Centres. The competition had three aims -

To teach Cub Scouts about the value and importance of water in everyday life.

To give Cub Scouts the opportunity to be creative and have fun.

To raise money for the charity, Water Aid.

Live On Stage - The 100th Viewforth & 134th Slateford Cub Scout Pack

THE CHALLENGE

The 10,500 Cub Scout Packs in England, Wales, Scotland and Northern Ireland were each sent an Activity Kit containing full details of the competition. The kit contained five different topics about water which could be investigated:

The Future World - becoming more aware of the water we use and how to save it.

The Leisure Park - realising the ways in which we can enjoy water safely.

The Global Zone - finding out how we can help people who have not got a safe water supply.

The Supply Sector - learning about how water is collected, treated and transported to and from our homes.

The Green Land - finding out about water in nature.

Each Cub Scout Pack was invited to produce a 5-minute video, like a TV programme, showing the value of water in one or more of these categories. Any number of people, including grown-ups, could be involved in making this video - but only six Cub Scouts could actually appear on the screen.

Live On Stage - The 1st Baldock (Knights) Cub Scout Pack performing during the Grand Final

THE HEAT IS ON!

Approximately 200,000 Cub Scouts took part in the competition in one way or another and their finished videos were sent to Scout HQs in London, Belfast and Scotland for judging. After long deliberations, the judges decided on the winning teams from each region of the country. The winners of these heats were invited to stay at Baden-Powell House in London over the weekend of March 20-21, 1999, and perform their entries live in front of another panel of judges in the Grand Final.

The 100th Viewforth & 134th Slateford Cub Scout Pack

AND THE WINNER IS ...

A total of six Cub Scout Packs took part in the Final on March 21st, just one day before World Water Day which aimed to highlight the enormous waste of water around the world. The standard of presentation was very high and the judges had a different task, but in the end they decided to award first prize to the 15th Huddersfield North Cub Scout Pack.

The colourful and imaginative show was performed on the day by:

Oliver Walshaw

Andrew Wejrowski

Felix Wisdom

Alex Bostrum

Thomas Raif

and

Jonathan Hird

For their excellent efforts, the boys received a cheque for £1,000 for a trip for their whole pack to a holiday destination of their choice. The 'Waterwise' competition as a whole raised a fantastic £22,000 for Water Aid and, at the end of the final, the Cub Scouts proudly gave a cheque for this amount to the chairman of the charity.

The Winners - The performing members of the 15th Huddersfield North Cub Scout Pack with their cheque for the first prize

107

Onward And Upward!

The Lowdown On Becoming A Scout

Just as you once outgrew the Beaver Scouts and left them behind, there will come a time around the age of 10 or 11 when you'll think about leaving the Cub Scouts and moving on to the third stage of the great Family of Scouts - the Scouts themselves.

The Same ... Yet Different

There is nothing to be afraid of about making this move. You will find many things are similar to the Cub Scouts.
For example:

You will still play games and meet regularly (possibly in the same Scout hut.)

You will make the same greetings and Scout Sign.
You will see the familiar World Membership Badge being worn and you will be allowed to wear the highest award you gained at Cub Scouts until you gain your Scout Membership Badge.

At the same time, of course, other things will be very different. You will no longer belong to a Cub Scout Pack - instead, you will be part of a Scout Troop. You will be expected to act in a more grown-up way and, as a result, you will be invited to take part in more grown-up (and exciting) activities such as Patrol projects, pioneering and camping expeditions. There is almost no limit to the fascinating and fun things you can find to do when you're a Scout!

The Scout Membership Badge

You can begin working for this first Scout award whilst you are in your final months as a Cub.

Here's what you have to do ...

Talk with your future Patrol Leader about joining the Troop.

Join a Patrol of your liking and get to know the other members by taking part in an activity with them.

Get to know the other Scouts and Leaders in the Troop by taking part in at least three Troop Meetings, one of which should be out of doors.

Show a general knowledge of the Scout Movement and the development of world wide Scouting.

Know, understand and accept the Scout Promise and Law. Talk with a Scout Leader and about how you can put them into practice each day.

Know what to do at your investiture and, if you would like to, invite someone to be there.

And remember – you must be over 10 years old to begin this award and every section has to be completed.

To help you get started, here are the two items which you need to fully understand and know by heart ...

The Scout Promise

On my honour, I promise that I will do my best to do my duty to God and to the Queen, to help other people and to keep the Scout Law.

The Scout Law

A Scout is to be trusted.
A Scout is loyal.
A Scout is friendly and considerate.
A Scout belongs to the world-wide family of Scouts.
A Scout has courage in all difficulties
A Scout makes good use of time and is careful of possessions and property.
A Scout has self-respect and respect for others.

Why not start learning them now?

And Finally ...

Onward And Upward!

When your time in the Beaver Colony comes to an end, it's time to move on to the next stage in the life of a Scout - becoming a Cub Scout.

Years ago, when Lord Baden-Powell set up this section of young Scouts, they were known as 'Wolf Cubs'. Though the name has now been changed to Cub Scouts, the connection with wolves remains. A large group of Cubs is knows as a 'Pack' and, when they greet their leader, they perform the 'Grand Howl'. This noisy greeting is great fun and something you can look forward to doing as a Cub.

Obviously, as you are now older and with more grown-up friends, the things you do at Cubs are even more exciting and enjoyable than at the Beavers. Here's a few ideas about what Cubs get up to ...

Play games
Gain badges
Make a special promise
Learn to look after themselves
Go on outings and visits
Go camping and learn about the great outdoors